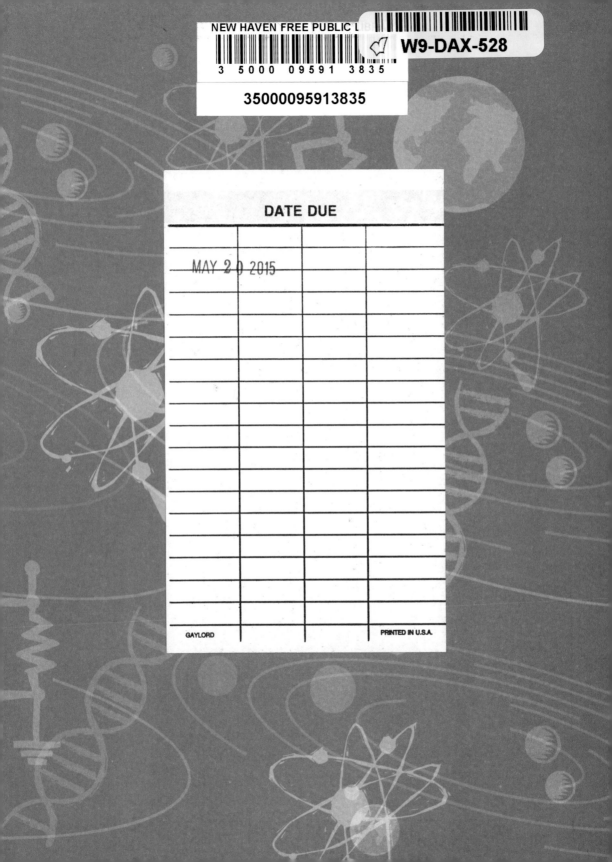

Alfred Wegener:

Pioneer of Plate Tectonics

by Greg Young

Science Contributor
Sally Ride Science
Science Consultants
Nancy McKeown, Planetary Geologist
William B. Rice, Engineering Geologist

First hardcover edition published in 2009 by
Compass Point Books
151 Good Counsel Drive
P.O. Box 669
Mankato, MN 56002-0669

Editor: Jennifer VanVoorst
Designer: Bobbie Nuytten
Editorial Contributor: Sue Vander Hook

Art Director: LuAnn Ascheman-Adams
Creative Director: Joe Ewest
Editorial Director: Nick Healy
Managing Editor: Catherine Neitge

 This book was manufactured with paper containing at least 10 percent post-consumer waste.

Library of Congress Cataloging-in-Publication Data
Young, Greg, 1968–
  Alfred Wegener : pioneer of plate tectonics / by Greg Young.—
  1st hardcover ed.
    p. cm. — (Mission: Science)
  Includes index.
  ISBN 978-0-7565-4233-7 (library binding)
1. Wegener, Alfred, 1880–1930—Juvenile literature.
2. Geologists—Germany—Biography—Juvenile literature.
3. Plate tectonics. I. Title. II. Series.
  QE22.W26Y675 2009
  550.92—dc22 [B]   2009013057

Visit Compass Point Books on the Internet at *www.compasspointbooks.com*
or e-mail your request to *custserv@compasspointbooks.com*

Table of Contents

Puzzle Pieces

Alfred Wegener's theory of continental drift changed the world of science. But it wasn't popular when he first talked about it in the early 1900s. Few scientists agreed with him that Earth's seven continents had once been a single large landmass that had slowly broken apart and drifted to new locations. But Wegener was convinced that his theory was correct, and he spent much of his life writing and teaching about drifting continents.

Wegener, a German meteorologist and geologist, first formed his theory while looking at a world map. He noticed that the eastern coastline of South America looked as if it would fit with the western coastline of Africa, much like interlocking puzzle pieces. He observed that other continents also looked as if they would fit together like parts of a giant jigsaw puzzle.

Other scientists noticed the puzzle pattern of the continents as well, but they thought it was merely a coincidence. Wegener believed it was something more, and he studied books, maps, fossils, and anything

Alfred Wegener spent a great deal of time trying to understand and prove his theory of continental drift.

else that might prove that his idea was based on fact.

Wegener wouldn't live long enough to see scientists accept his theory. He didn't know that his idea about drifting continents would one day support the theory of plate tectonics—that Earth's crust is made of huge slabs of rock that float on molten rock.

Many discoveries in the mid-1950s would provide the evidence Wegener had been looking for. New technology would show that the continents were indeed drifting slowly on pieces of Earth's crust. And evidence would show that the crust was floating on the mantle—a layer of molten

Wegener used fossils of plant and animal life to try to prove his theory.

rock between the planet's crust and core. Wegener would one day be highly respected for his idea, but it would be after his death at the age of 50.

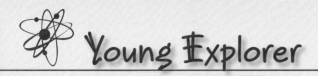
Alfred Lothar Wegener was born November 1, 1880, in Berlin, Germany. His father, Richard Wegener, was a minister who directed an orphanage. His mother, Anna Wegener, took care of the home and family.

As a young boy, Alfred became interested in Greenland, the world's largest island, located between the Arctic Ocean and the North Atlantic Ocean. He hiked, skated, and walked to become strong enough to be an explorer one day. Whenever he walked, he pretended he was on a great expedition.

When Alfred was old enough to go to college, he attended the University of Berlin, where he studied astronomy. In 1904 he

Alfred Wegener

received a Ph.D., the highest degree a student can earn. He found, however, that he liked learning about Earth more than about outer space. He especially became fascinated with meteorology, the study of weather and climate.

Wegener still wanted to explore. He especially wanted to travel to Greenland. And he also became interested in flying, particularly in a hot air balloon.

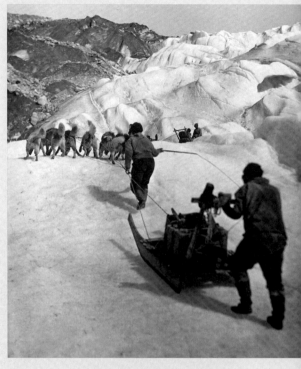

Greenland's cold climate and forbidding terrain make it a challenge for explorers.

Did You Know?

Greenland is a very large island with an area of about 836,000 square miles (2.17 million square kilometers). It is the largest landmass to be called an island rather than a continent. About 80 percent of Greenland is covered with ice. Vikings from Iceland came to the island in the 10th century. The Inuit had already been living there for centuries.

Alfred Wegener and his brother, Kurt, were both interested in hot air balloons and kites. In 1906 they won a hot air balloon contest, setting a world record for flying 52 hours. Wegener used his experience with balloons to pioneer the use of weather balloons to track air circulation and study the weather.

That same year, Wegener's childhood dream came true: He went to Greenland. He was invited to explore the island because of his record-setting balloon flight and his contributions to

First Hot Air Balloon

Two French brothers, Joseph-Michel Montgolfier and Jacques-Étienne Montgolfier, are credited with making the first hot air balloon. On September 19, 1783, the brothers placed a duck, a chicken, and a sheep inside the basket of their balloon. The 2-mile (3-km) flight over the royal palace in Versailles lasted about eight minutes before the craft landed safely. On November 21 of that year, the first humans took flight in a hot air balloon, and an exciting new sport was born.

The first hot air balloons used burning straw and manure to heat the air inside the balloon in order to make it rise. Today hot air balloons use propane gas. A hot air balloon doesn't have an engine or a motor, and it doesn't need electricity. It works because a propane gas burner warms the air inside the balloon, making it less dense than the cold air outside. This causes the balloon to rise.

weather kite from the early 1900s

Kite Science

In 1749 Alexander Wilson and Thomas Melvill, two scientists at the University of Glasgow, Scotland, tied thermometers to a series of kites and released them into the air. They wanted to know whether the air up high was colder or warmer than the air near the ground. As soon as the kites and thermometers came down, the scientists recorded the temperatures of the air at various altitudes. Their experiment showed that kites could be used to obtain information about the weather.

meteorology. As the official meteorologist for the trip, he used kites and balloons to study weather in the Arctic. Meteorology was a good fit with Wegener's interests.

When Wegener returned from Greenland, he accepted a teaching position at the University of Marburg in Germany, where he taught meteorology. He also wrote a book, *The Thermodynamics of the Atmosphere*, which became the standard meteorology textbook in Germany.

Wegener became well known for his book and his work in meteorology. He was well-liked by his students and fellow teachers. They thought he was full of great ideas. It was at the University of Marburg that Wegener developed his most famous idea: the theory of continental drift.

giant panda

Syrian brown bear

polar bear

American black bear

European brown bear

While browsing through books at the University of Marburg library, Wegener read about a strange occurrence. Identical plant and animal fossils had been found on opposite sides of the Atlantic Ocean. Wegener investigated further and found other places where matching fossils were separated by large bodies of water.

Then as Wegener was studying a map of the world, he noticed that the coast of western Africa looked as if it could fit with the eastern coast of South America. He wondered whether the continents had once been joined as one large landmass and then separated over time. That would explain how identical fossils were found on both continents. He called his idea the theory of continental drift and publicly proposed it in 1912. He believed his theory was sound, but he knew he would need evidence to back it up.

◄ Bears are found on several continents around the globe.

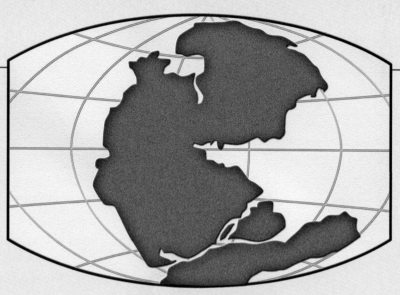

Wegener's name for a giant supercontinent, Pangaea, means "entire Earth."

PERMIAN PERIOD
225 MILLION YEARS AGO

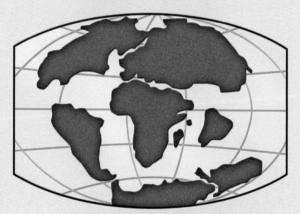

CRETACEOUS PERIOD
65 MILLION YEARS AGO

PRESENT DAY

Scientific Theories

A scientific idea is called a theory. Theories take time to develop and require a great deal of evidence before they are accepted or rejected. Theories are confirmed or disproved through many tests. Even if a theory is accepted, it is still open to debate. More evidence might challenge the theory. Many accepted theories are later rejected after a better explanation is found.

13

Wegener traveled to Greenland again in 1912. He participated in the longest crossing of the ice cap ever made on foot. It was a very dangerous trip, and he and three other explorers almost died when a glacier on which they were climbing broke loose. They had to spend the entire winter on the ice cap. Wegener used this time to collect information. He learned about storms over the Arctic and became an expert on Arctic meteorology.

When Wegener returned from Greenland, he married Else Köppen, whom he had met five years earlier. Else was the daughter of well-known meteorologist Wladimir Köppen. She had moved to Norway while Wegener was exploring

▲ Else Köppen

◀ Wegener's travels in Greenland helped him become one of the world's most knowledgeable experts on the Arctic.

Greenland in order to be closer to him. Alfred and Else would eventually have three daughters.

In 1914 Wegener served in World War I. But after being injured twice, he was released from combat duty and assigned to work with the German army's weather forecasting service. Wegener then took a position his father-in-law had once held—director of the meteorological research department of the Marine Observatory in Hamburg, Germany. As part of his job, Wegener studied craters on the moon. He tried to

Thinking Ahead

Weather forecasting is the attempt to identify weather before it happens. People once tried to predict the weather by watching cloud patterns or using astrology. Today meteorologists use weather satellites, radar, and computers to help predict the weather.

recreate these craters on Earth, and the results of his experiments suggested that the craters were likely the result of something's hitting them. The papers he wrote about his experiments made him quite well known.

Did You Know?

The Alfred Wegener Institute in Bremerhaven, Germany, conducts polar and marine research. It carries on Wegener's work, conducting Arctic research and assisting polar expeditions.

In 1915 Alfred Wegener wrote *The Origin of Continents and Oceans*, a book that explained his theory of a supercontinent. He claimed that about 300 million years ago the continents were one mass of land—a giant continent he called Pangaea. He proposed that Pangaea eventually broke apart and that the pieces had been moving apart ever since.

Wegener thought two forces caused Pangaea to break apart and start drifting. The first was centrifugal force—caused by the spinning of Earth—which pulled the continents toward the equator. The second force was gravity—the gravity of the sun and moon pulling on Earth. Wegener suggested that the continents had moved across the ocean floor like ships plowing through

How Many Continents?

In the United States, students are taught that there are seven continents—Africa, Antarctica, Asia, Australia, Europe, North America, and South America. In other parts of the world, students learn that there are only six. Sometimes North and South America are combined and called the Americas. Some schools teach that Europe and Asia are one continent called Eurasia. Since *continent* is defined as a large landmass, there is a lot of disagreement over how to divide Earth's large pieces of land.

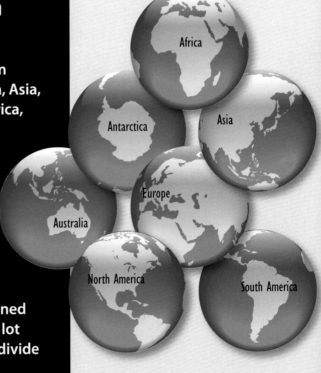

Africa

Antarctica

Asia

Europe

Australia

North America

South America

sheets of ice. He had seen ships do this in the icy waters of the Arctic Ocean.

Most geologists of Wegener's time rejected his explanation and his theory. They didn't believe that centrifugal force and gravity were strong enough to move huge continents. They thought the Earth's crust was too hard for masses of land to simply plow through it. Scientists would eventually prove that Wegener's theory was correct, but his explanation about the two forces was not.

Geologists Rock!

Geologists study the origin and structure of Earth. They also investigate the forces that change our planet and the effects they have on people. They examine what lies under Earth's crust, as well as what is in it and above it. Rocks hold many clues to the history of our planet. They also provide ways for geologists to predict volcanoes, earthquakes, and lava flows. Geologists often try to unravel mysteries of our planet, such as why fossils of marine animals can be found on top of Mount Everest. They search for oil, water, and gas and try to predict earthquakes and tsunamis.

Many geologists didn't believe Wegener had a good explanation for how the continents had moved. Some of them came up with another explanation for the misplaced fossils. They suggested that at one time the continents had been connected by land bridges, which allowed plants and animals to migrate from one landmass to another. They believed the land bridges were now sunk beneath the ocean. Today we know that although there were some land bridges on the planet, there weren't enough to explain all of the fossil similarities.

Wegener used his experience as a meteorologist to try to prove his theory of continental drift. He knew that some types of animals and plants could not have survived the climate in the area where their fossils were found. Animals and plants found in Antarctica could never have endured the cold. He concluded that they must have come from a place closer to the equator.

In the meantime, Wegener continued to explore and study Greenland. On his fourth trip to the island, he studied the jet stream, the swift air currents that encircle Earth and usually flow from west to east.

Rich Source of Coal

Coal is a hard black or dark brown rock formed underground long ago from decayed plants. For centuries it has been mined and used as a source of fuel. Pennsylvania has an abundant source of coal that was formed from decayed tropical plants. How did tropical plants grow in a state that does not have a tropical climate? It is believed that Pennsylvania was once located close to the equator and had a hot, humid climate. The state's rich coal supply is one piece of evidence used today to prove the theory of continental drift.

Jet Stream

The jet stream is like a river of wind in the atmosphere. It is about 4 to 6 miles (6 to 9 km) above Earth's surface. The jet stream helps move storms around the planet. In the Northern Hemisphere, the jet stream travels from west to east. A plane flying from California to New York is pushed by the jet stream and travels more quickly to its destination than a plane traveling in the opposite direction. One flying from New York to California is slowed down by the jet stream.

Jet streams are usually in Earth's Northern Hemisphere in places such as Greenland, where Alfred Wegener was studying them. During very cold weather, they can travel south, taking storms with them.

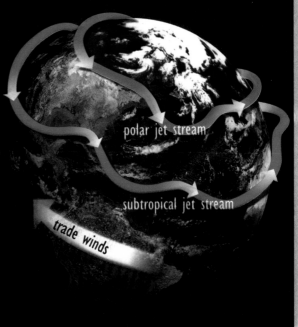

polar jet stream

subtropical jet stream

trade winds

While there he celebrated his 50th birthday. But then tragedy struck. The next day, November 2, 1930, Wegener delivered supplies to a scientific research station. Then Wegener and a fellow scientist went missing. They never returned to the base camp. The harsh winter weather was most likely to blame for the disappearance and deaths of the two men.

Wegener's wife, Else, was deeply saddened by his death. She wrote a book in memory of her husband and his work. Else Wegener-Köppen died in 1992 at the age of 100.

After Alfred Wegener's death, his theory of continental drift was largely ignored—until scientists noticed that Earth's crust might be spreading. In the mid-1900s, geologists studied and mapped the ocean floor. They discovered an underwater mountain range, which they found had a valley down the center of it. On each side were mountain peaks. Magma was seeping up through the crack, forming new seafloor that most likely was pushing the ridge farther apart. If the seafloor was in

Marie Tharp
(1920—2006)

Marie Tharp began her work as a geologist during World War II. Since so many men had been sent off to war, women had new opportunities, and Tharp was recruited by the University of Michigan to study in its geology department. After graduating with honors, Tharp continued her research of the ocean floor.

Using sonar data, she drew what the floor of the North Atlantic Ocean probably looked like. In 1977 she published a map depicting the terrain of the entire seafloor, with its vast plains, deep canyons, and soaring mountain peaks. Her discovery of a valley in the middle of the Mid-Atlantic Ridge led scientists to propose the idea of seafloor spreading, which in turn encouraged scientists to consider Wegener's theory of continental drift.

In 1978 Tharp and her research partner, Bruce Heezen, received the National Geographic Society's Hubbard Medal for their research.

fact moving, then Wegener's theory of continental drift might be true, and the continents might be moving, too.

Harry Hammond Hess [1906—1969]

Harry Hammond Hess is considered one of the founding fathers of plate tectonics. He was a geology teacher until he joined the U.S. Navy during World War II. While moving between battles in the Pacific Ocean, he used his ship's sonar equipment to study the ocean floor. He discovered underwater volcanoes, which led to his important 1960 report on seafloor spreading, formally published two years later as *History of Ocean Basins*.

Hess' findings confirmed Wegener's theory of continental drift. Hess agreed with what Wegener had proposed, although he didn't agree with Wegener about how the continents moved. After Hess' death in 1969, he was awarded NASA's Distinguished Public Service Award for his significant work.

Scientists called their findings about moving continents the theory of plate tectonics. They suggested that Earth's crust is made up of huge slabs of rock that float on hot, molten magma. The plates move very slowly, a movement that is not noticeable to humans. However, now and then the plates collide.

The edges of the plates—called plate boundaries—sometimes scrape or crash into each other. Other times a plate gets wedged underneath another plate. When plates run into each other, the results are often noticeable. There is often a volcano or an earthquake.

The flow of molten magma under the planet's crust pushes and pulls the plates above.

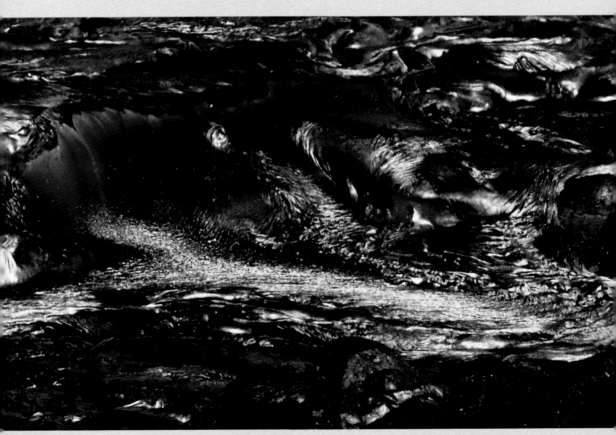

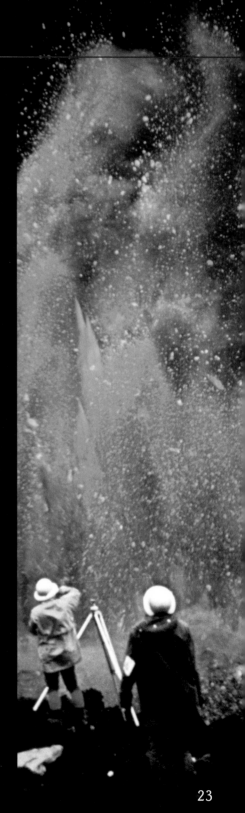

Volcanologists

Today we use plate tectonics—or the movement of Earth's plates—to explain earthquakes and volcanoes. This has opened up new areas of science, such as the study of volcanoes. Scientists who study volcanoes are called volcanologists.

Janet Sumner is a volcanologist who investigates active volcanoes and examines lava samples. She studies how volcanoes are linked to plate movements. Most volcanoes occur in the gap between plate boundaries or where one plate is being pushed under another plate. Hot molten magma bubbles up to the surface and eventually seeps out or explodes as a volcano.

Sumner is especially interested in volcanic fire-fountain eruptions. Lava from these fountains is very dangerous. It is fast-flowing and can travel great distances. She has found that syrup and candle wax behave a lot like magma. Using these liquids, she discovered how clots of magma produce lava.

Alfred Wegener didn't know that plate tectonics causes volcanoes. But his work laid the foundation for what scientists such as Sumner have been able to discover.

Today we know that Earth's crust is made up of 14 large tectonic plates and many smaller ones. Some of the plates support continents, while others are under the ocean floor. These plates float around on Earth's upper mantle, the molten layer between the crust and the core. The layer consists of magma, which rises to the surface of Earth and seeps out where plates meet.

Volcanoes are not just spectacular displays of spurting lava erupting from a mountaintop. A volcano is any vent or opening in Earth's crust where magma, gases, hot water, rocks, or hot ash escape. Some vents are on the floor of the ocean. Others are under a mountain.

Earth's moving plates have created many geologic features.

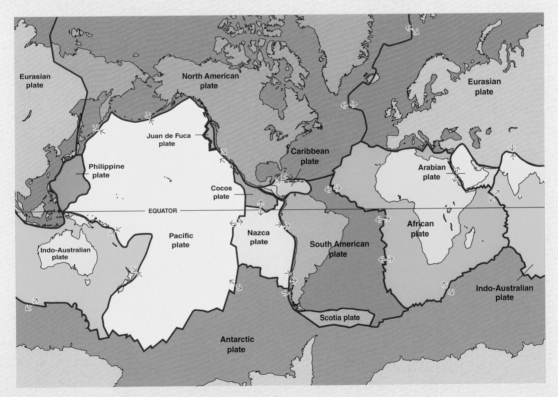

Mount St. Helens

In May 1980, the side of Mount St. Helens in Washington exploded. Huge evergreen trees, mud, and volcanic ash cascaded down the mountainside into Spirit Lake at the base of the mountain. Volcanologists had predicted the eruption months before, when earthquakes occurred and steam billowed forth.

The events began when the edge of the Juan de Fuca plate was pushed beneath the North American plate. The boundary of the Juan de Fuca plate melted in the heat of the mantle and eventually spewed out through the crack between the two plates in the side of the mountain.

Alfred Wegener's theory of continental drift was the beginning of the science of plate tectonics. If Wegener had known about the planet's shifting plates, he might also have understood earthquakes. The constant slow movement of the plates is the cause of Earth's shaking and rumbling from time to time.

When tectonic plates make a sudden movement, an earthquake can result. Two plates scraping past each other might get hung up on jagged rock. When the rock breaks loose, the ground

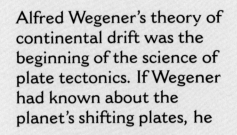

◀ Alfred Wegener

The discovery of oceanic mountain ranges
▼ led to the acceptance of Wegener's ideas.

trembles. The more forceful the movement, the more powerful the earthquake. On rare occasions, an earthquake occurs in the middle of a tectonic plate. Scientists are still studying what triggers these earthquakes.

What Wegener needed to prove his theory was not discovered until the mid-1900s, when scientists finally found enough evidence to explain the movement of the continents. Modern scientists, equipped with new technology, were able to map the ocean floor and explore deep into Earth's crust. Wegener didn't live long enough to make these discoveries himself. But scientists used Wegener's foundation to develop their own work. That is the nature of science: The work of one scientist builds upon the work of others. In the future, scientists are sure to learn more and more and to advance the work that Alfred Wegener began.

ALFRED WEGENER 1880 1930

GRÜNLAND FORSCHER

S4

REPUBLIK ÖSTERREICH

A. PILCH   1980   W. PFEILER

Wegener's picture has appeared on many postage stamps, including a stamp from Austria.

Geophysicist: Mary Lou Zoback

Western Earthquake Hazards Team (U.S. Geological Survey)

Shake, Rattle, and Roll

Mary Lou Zoback is a research scientist with the U.S. Geological Survey's Earthquake Hazards Team. She studies tectonic plates and the relationship between earthquakes and stress on the planet's crust. She has focused her research on the hazards of earthquakes in the San Francisco Bay area of California, where the devastating earthquake of 1906 set off fires that caused hundreds of deaths and where other major earthquakes have occurred.

Zoback's interest in geophysics, the study of Earth's physical characteristics, was sparked by one of her college professors. She became interested in how the surface of Earth moves and how those movements cause earthquakes. In 1978 Zoback received her doctorate in geophysics from Stanford University in California.

Zoback's goal is to predict earthquakes. She uses instruments that measure how much the ground shakes during an earthquake. She also uses information from satellites, which measure the surface of Earth from space.

Zoback's favorite parts of her work are the surprises. "Often you look for one thing and something else completely different will jump out at you," she says. "That's the fun part of science."

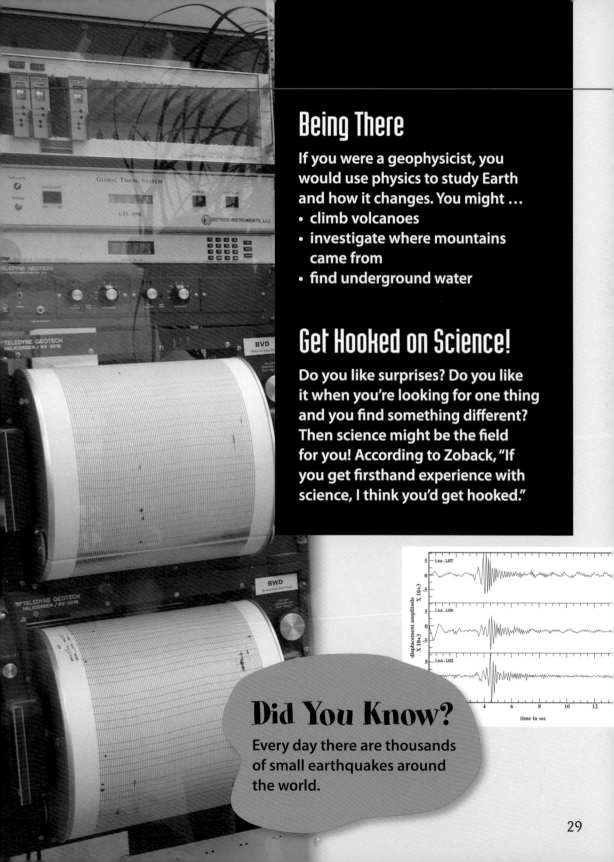

Being There

If you were a geophysicist, you would use physics to study Earth and how it changes. You might ...

- climb volcanoes
- investigate where mountains came from
- find underground water

Get Hooked on Science!

Do you like surprises? Do you like it when you're looking for one thing and you find something different? Then science might be the field for you! According to Zoback, "If you get firsthand experience with science, I think you'd get hooked."

Did You Know?

Every day there are thousands of small earthquakes around the world.

Name:	Alfred Lothar Wegener
Date of birth:	November 1, 1880
Nationality:	German
Birthplace:	Berlin, Germany
Parents:	Richard and Anna Wegener
Spouse:	Else Wegener-Köppen
Children:	Three daughters
Fields of study:	Meteorology, geology
Known for:	Theory of continental drift
Contributions to science:	Established the theory of continental drift, which laid the foundation for the theory of plate tectonics
Awards and honors:	The Wegener Medal is awarded in his name by the Alfred Wegener Institute; the Wegener impact craters on Mars and the moon are named after him; asteroid 29227 Wegener is named after him; the Wegener Peninsula in Greenland, the place where he died, is named after him; the Alfred Wegener Medal & Honorary Membership, sponsored by the European Geosciences Union, is awarded to scientists who have achieved exceptional international standing in atmospheric, hydrological, or ocean sciences
Publications:	*The Thermodynamics of the Atmosphere; The Origin of Continents and Oceans*

Florence Bascom (1862–1945)
American geologist and one of the first female geologists; studied mountains and how they are formed

Samuel Warren Carey (1911–2002)
Australian geologist who was an early advocate of the theory of continental drift; developed the theory of the expanding Earth, which proposes that Earth's volume is increasing, causing the formation of tectonic plates

William Maurice Ewing (1906–1974)
American oceanographer who made detailed maps of the sea bottom using refraction of waves caused by explosions (similar to sonar); helped describe the Mid-Atlantic Ridge, an area of spreading seafloor in the Atlantic Ocean

Beno Gutenberg (1889–1960)
German-American geologist who determined the boundary between Earth's mantle and core, based on the behavior of earthquake waves

Harry Hammond Hess (1906–1969)
American geologist who developed the theory of seafloor spreading, in which new crust develops at mid-ocean ridges and is destroyed at deep sea trenches

Charles Francis Richter (1900–1985)
American seismologist who developed a scale for measuring the intensity of earthquakes, called the Richter scale

Marie Tharp (1920–2006)
American geologist who, with research partner Bruce Heezen, discovered a valley in the middle of the Mid-Atlantic Ridge and published a map of the entire ocean floor

1086	Chinese scientist Shen Kua's *Dream Pool Essays* describe the principles of erosion, uplift, and sedimentation—the foundations of Earth science
1620	English scientist Francis Bacon notices the jigsaw fit of opposite shores of the Atlantic Ocean
1743	Christopher Packe, an English physician and geologist, makes a geological map of the southeast portion of England
1760	English geologist John Michell suggests that earthquakes are caused by one layer of rocks rubbing against another
1785	Scottish geologist James Hutton presents his study *Theory of the Earth*, in which he suggests that Earth is very old
1809	William Maclure, called the father of American geology, completes the first geological survey of the eastern United States
1815	English geologist William Smith creates the first large-scale geological map of England and Wales; later wins the first Wollaston Medal for achievement in geology
1828	First measurement of Earth's magnetic field
1830	Scottish geologist Charles Lyell publishes his book *Principles of Geology*, in which he states that the world is several hundred million years old
1880	British seismologist and geologist John Milne invents the modern seismograph for measuring earthquake waves

1906	Earthquake waves are first used to determine Earth's layers
1907	American scientist Bertram Boltwood uses uranium to determine the age of rocks
1911	English geologist Arthur Holmes uses radioactivity to date rocks and states that Earth is 3 million years old
1912	Alfred Wegener proposes the theory of continental drift
1915	Wegener writes *The Origin of Continents and Oceans,* in which he argues for his theory of continental drift
1925	German expedition uses sonar to confirm the existence of the Mid-Atlantic Ridge, a mountainlike ridge through the Atlantic and Arctic oceans resulting from the separation of tectonic plates
1935	American seismologist Charles Francis Richter develops a scale to determine earthquake intensity
1950s	Scientists, including American geologist Harry Hammond Hess, discover odd magnetic variations across the ocean floor
1953	Team of geologists from Columbia University maps the Mid-Atlantic Ridge
1958	Australian geologist Samuel Warren Carey publishes *The Tectonic Approach to Continental Drift*, an essay in support of the expanding Earth theory

1960	Hess proposes the idea of seafloor spreading, lending credibility to Wegener's theory of continental drift
1968	French geophysicist Xavier Le Pichon publishes a complete model of Earth based on six major tectonic plates and their motions
1969	Core sample data from deep sea research vessel *Glomar Challenger* provides conclusive evidence for seafloor spreading and, as a result, continental drift
1977	American oceanographers John Corliss and Robert Ballard discover deep-sea vents around the Galapagos Islands in the Pacific Ocean; American geologists Marie Tharp and Bruce Heezen publish a map showing the geologic features of the entire ocean floor
1985	American oceanographer Peter Rona finds the first deep-sea vents in the Atlantic Ocean
1990	Oldest portion of the Pacific plate is found
2007	American geologist Vicki Hansen proposes that early meteorites created the first cracks in Earth's crust, which she says jump-started the movement of Earth's tectonic plates
2009	German scientists create a mathematical model for calculating the future position of continents

Glossary

astrology—belief that the positions of stars and planets influence human affairs

astronomy—study of the universe and of objects in space such as the moon, sun, planets, and stars

centrifugal force—force felt by an object moving in a curved path that pulls the object outward away from the center of rotation

continent—single large area of land

continental drift—theory that continents move from one place to another by the motion of gigantic plates that make up Earth's crust

crater—bowl-shaped cavity made by the impact of an object such as a meteoroid

crust—Earth's thin outer layer of rock

earthquake—sudden movement of Earth's crust caused by volcanic activity or the release of stress along plate boundaries

equator—imaginary line around the middle of Earth at an equal distance from the two poles

fossils—remains of ancient plants or animals that have hardened into rock; also the preserved tracks or outlines of ancient organisms

geologist—scientist who studies how Earth formed and how it changes by examining soil, rocks, rivers, and other landforms

geology—study of how Earth was formed and how it changes

geophysics—study of Earth's properties using physical principles

glacier—large mass of slowly moving ice

gravity—force of attraction between two objects

hypothesis—scientific prediction about what will happen in an experiment

ice cap—coverings of ice at the North and South poles

jet stream—high-speed wind current, usually moving from west to east

land bridge—stretch of land that connects two landmasses

landmass—large unbroken area of land

lava—magma that comes out of a volcano

magma—hot, molten rock beneath Earth's crust

mantle—layer of hot rock between Earth's crust and core

meteorologist—scientist who studies weather and climate

meteorology—scientific study of Earth's atmosphere, especially weather conditions

Mid-Atlantic Ridge—area of seafloor in the Atlantic Ocean that is spreading apart

Pangaea—single landmass made of all of today's continents; means "entire Earth"

plate boundaries—edges of plates, which sometimes scrape or collide with each other

plate tectonics—theory that Earth's crust is made up of large slabs of rock that move about on molten magma

satellites—objects that move around a planet or other cosmic body

seafloor spreading—process by which new oceanic crust is formed by the seeping up of magma at mid-ocean ridges

sonar—device that measures the distance to an object by bouncing sound waves off the object and timing how long it takes the waves to return

tectonic plates—gigantic slabs of Earth's crust that move around on magma

theory—system of ideas intended to explain observations

tsunami—gigantic ocean wave created by an undersea earthquake, landslide, or volcanic eruption

vent—opening on the ocean floor that releases magma, hot water, and volcanic material

volcano—vent in Earth's crust from which lava pours; mountain formed from the buildup of lava

volcanologist—scientist who studies volcanoes

weather balloons—high-altitude balloons that carry instruments to collect and transmit weather data

Additional Resources

Edwards, John. *Plate Tectonics and Continental Drift.* North Mankato, Minn.: Smart Apple Media, 2006.

Rubin, Ken. *Volcanoes & Earthquakes.* New York: Simon & Schuster Children's Publishing, 2007.

Stille, Darlene. *Great Shakes: The Science of Earthquakes.* Minneapolis: Compass Point Books, 2009.

Van Gorp, Lynn. *Landforms.* Minneapolis: Compass Point Books, 2010.

Yount, Lisa. *Alfred Wegener: Creator of the Continental Drift Theory.* New York: Chelsea House, 2009.

Internet Sites

FactHound offers a safe, fun way to find Internet sites related to this book. All of the sites on FactHound have been researched by our staff.

Here's all you do:

Visit *www.facthound.com*

FactHound will fetch the best sites for you!

Index

Greg Young

Greg Young has been a high school chemistry and physics teacher for 18 years. He enjoys sharing his interest in Earth science with his students. By demonstrating how the periodic table relates to mineralogy and the star life cycle and how Newtonian physics relates to satellites and moon phases, he provides students practical examples of the concepts they are learning. Practical examples are the "hook" in teaching science at any grade level.

Image Credits